The ancient village of Peach Blossom lay on a narrow strip of land between Eagle Mountain and the Po River. The only way in or out of Peach Blossom Village was by climbing a steep path over the mountain or crossing the river on Dragon Bridge. Most people used Dragon Bridge because it saved them time and energy. The bridge was handsomely constructed from an odd-looking stone. It had stood for as long as anyone could remember. Not even the village elder, Old Lee, knew how long Dragon Bridge had been there or who had built it.

Life in Peach Blossom Village was easy and peaceful. Most of the village folk were farmers who grew peaches and almonds in the green hills surrounding the village. During the cool, sunny days of mid-autumn, the farmers harvested their peaches and almonds. They loaded them into baskets, placed the baskets on donkey carts, and drove them over Dragon Bridge to the neighboring town. There they sold their harvest at the market or traded for things they needed. And so things had gone for a very long time.

座落在大鹰山和宝河之间有个古老的村落叫做桃花村。如果想要进出桃花村，必须靠爬过窄小的山路或越过河上的龙桥。为了节省时间和精力，村民们大都选择通过龙桥出入村庄。这座俊美的桥是用一种奇特的石头打造而成，远自老祖先们有记忆以来，龙桥就已经座落在那里。甚至村里年纪最大的李长老都不知道这座桥是在何时或由谁建造的。

桃花村的生活很安详，大部分的居民以农耕维生。 他们在环绕着村落的山丘上种植桃子和杏仁。农夫们会在凉爽的中秋艳阳天中收割他们的农作物，然后这些桃子和杏仁会被装进篮子，载上驴车，越过龙桥，运送到邻近城镇的市集里贩售，或换取生活必需品。长久以来他们一直都维持着这样的生活方式 。

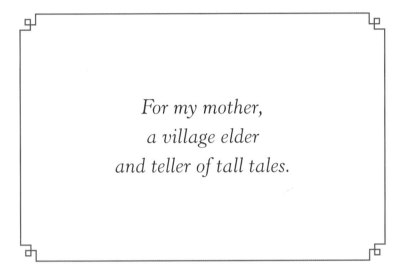

For my mother,
a village elder
and teller of tall tales.

Published by
North Atlantic Books
P.O. Box 12327
Berkeley, California 94712

Artwork by Ann Howard
Cover and book design by Susan Quasha
Printed in the United States of America

The Mystery of Dragon Bridge: A Peach Blossom Village Story is sponsored by the Society for the Study of Native Arts and Sciences, a nonprofit educational corporation whose goals are to develop an educational and cross-cultural perspective linking various scientific, social, and artistic fields; to nurture a holistic view of arts, sciences, humanities, and healing; and to publish and distribute literature on the relationship of mind, body, and nature.

North Atlantic Books' publications are available through most bookstores. For further information, visit our website at www.northatlanticbooks.com or call 800–733–3000.

ISBN-13: 978-1-58394-813-2

Library of Congress Control Number: 2014940569

1 2 3 4 5 6 7 8 9 VERSA 19 18 17 16 15 14

The Mystery of Dragon Bridge

龍橋之謎

A Peach Blossom Village Story
桃花村的故事之一

written and illustrated by
Ann Howard

North Atlantic Books
Berkeley, California

But one particular morning in early autumn, just before harvest season, the villagers were awakened by a great hue and cry. They looked out their windows and saw their people racing about the streets shouting, "It's gone! It's gone!" Gone? What was gone? There was so much confusion that the village elder, Old Lee, called for everyone to assemble for an emergency meeting in the great hall.

然而在即将收成前，一个初秋的清晨，桃花村的村民们在阵阵吵杂声中醒来，因为窗外有人在街上狂奔大喊：「不见了！不见了！」不见了吗？是什么东西不见了？大家一头雾水，于是李长老要大家到大厅集合，并召开紧急会议。

As he sat before the bewildered villagers, Old Lee announced that Dragon Bridge was gone—it had simply vanished in the night. No one knew quite what to say. After all, how could a bridge just disappear? More importantly, it was nearly harvest time. How could they take their crops to market? The Po River, swollen by recent rains, was much too wide and fast to cross safely in their small boats. And the old path over Eagle Mountain was too steep and narrow to carry heavy baskets of peaches and almonds to market. Some of the villagers shouted that they must build a new bridge. Yes, that would have to be done, indeed. But there was no time to finish a new bridge before the harvest.

Finally, Old Lee turned to Master Chen and asked him for his help. Master Chen had been a soldier and had traveled far and wide. He was known to be both brave and intelligent. Without hesitation, he agreed to go investigate what had happened to their bridge.

李长老坐在一群惊慌的村民面前宣布，龙桥真的不见了它就在一夜间消失了！没有人知道该说些什么，毕竟一座这么大的桥怎可能凭空消失？最重要的是，收成的时间已快到了，他们将如何运送农获去市集？由于最近多雨，宝河已涨满了水，如果用小船来横渡又宽又急的宝河，实在太危险。若以满载桃子和杏仁的驴车，越过大鹰山陡斜又狭窄的山路去市场，更是困难。有些村民叫着说该造一座新桥，是阿！那是必然的，但是已经没有时间在收成前完成一座新桥了。

最后，李长老转向陈师傅，请他帮忙。陈师傅曾经从过军，并且云遊過四方，而且他的勇气与智慧是众所皆知的。陈师傅毫不迟疑，马上答应去调查龙桥在一夜间消失之谜。

Master Chen walked down to the riverbank, followed by Old Lee and a group of curious villagers. He came to the spot where the bridge had once stood and began looking around. Master Chen soon found some colorful, flat stones that looked a bit like giant fish scales. He also found some very strange-looking footprints nearby. The tracks led away from the river toward Eagle Mountain. Master Chen put the strange, shiny stones into his pack and began following the tracks. He followed them for most of the morning. All along the way he found more and more of the odd-looking stones.

陈师傅後面跟著李长老和一群好奇的村民，一起来到宝河岸边。他开始在曾经座落着龙桥的地点四处探寻，很快地，他就找到一些类似鱼麟的彩色石片。接着，他又发现一些奇怪的脚印，这些脚印似乎是朝向大鹰山而去。陈师傅把石片放进他的口袋后，便开始循着脚印往大鹰山走去。他几乎走了整着早上，一路上又发现更多同样的奇怪石片。

As Master Chen was nearing the top of Eagle Mountain, the tracks suddenly disappeared into the mouth of a large and very dark cave. Master Chen walked up to the opening of the cave and called out, "Hello! Is anyone there?" After a few moments he heard heavy thumping noises and was startled when the huge head of a dragon suddenly came poking out of the cave. "What do you want from me?" thundered the magnificent but rather bedraggled-looking beast. Master Chen bowed to the great dragon and told him about the missing bridge. He then asked him politely if he had any idea what had happened to it. The dragon's face fell and he suddenly looked very sad. He heaved a heavy sigh and said, "I was Dragon Bridge." Master Chen was amazed by this. "How is that possible?" he asked. So the dragon told him a most curious tale.

当他快爬到山顶时，脚印突然消失在一个又大又黑的山洞前。陈师傅走到山洞口，大声喊道：「喂！有人在吗？」随后，他先听到沉重的脚步声，然后一颗巨大的龙头探出洞外！他吓了一跳！这只雄伟，却看起来很狼狈的怪兽，以打雷似的声音问：「你找我做什么？」陈师傅对着巨龙深深一鞠躬，然后对它说明龙桥消失的事，并用很有貌的口气问它是否知道龙桥那里去了。听完之后，巨龙低下头，表情变得很难过。 它深深叹一口气说道：「我就是龙桥！」 陈师傅很惊讶地问道 ：「 这怎么可能 ？」于是巨龙告诉他一个最不可思议的故事。

Around three hundred years ago, the old stone bridge that stretched over the Po River was destroyed in a great flood. The dragon, who was very fond of watching the leisurely comings and goings of the little village, felt great pity for its people. So he came up with an ingenious plan. You see, every thousand years or so, dragons go into a five-hundred-year-long hibernation. Since the time for his great sleep was growing near, the dragon decided to transform himself into a bridge and serve the villagers during his long nap. And so he did.

远在三百年前，横跨宝河的老石桥被洪水冲毁了。巨龙说它一直很爱旁观桃花村村民进进出出的悠闲生活，当时很同情他们的处境，于是他想到一个很好的计画。因为所有的巨龙每过一千年都要沉睡五百年。刚好它的冬眠期也快到了，它决定将自己变成一座桥来帮助村民，而且它真的做到了。

At that point, Master Chen interrupted him. "Why did you wake up two hundred years too early?" The dragon sighed, once again, and told him that he had no choice. The villagers no longer cared for him as they used to. In the beginning, he said, they held an annual Dragon Festival to honor him and show their appreciation. During the celebration the women and children of the village would drape flowers on him, and the men would clean and polish his stony scales.

陈师傅此时打断他的话，问道：「那你为何提早两百年醒来？」巨龙再次叹了一大口气，说他是万不得已的，因为随着时间久了，村民们已渐渐忘记它的重要性。 很久以前，他们曾经以巨龙为荣耀，制订了一年一度的节庆日来表达他们对它的感激 。 在节庆日那天，妇人和孩子们会用鲜花来装饰它，然后男人们会清洗，并擦亮它石样的麟片。

But with the passing of years, he began to look less and less like a dragon and more and more like an old stone bridge. The villagers' grandchildren came to believe the tale of Dragon Bridge was just a fable. Over time, their grandchildren forgot the story completely and finally stopped holding the festival altogether. As decades passed, the bridge became so encrusted with moss and river mud that no one would ever imagine there was a dragon underneath it at all.

After three hundred years had passed, the dragon awoke to a terrible itching and burning deep within his scales. He had been so neglected by the villagers that he was becoming ill. He realized that the people of Peach Blossom, who had once revered him, were now taking him for granted. The dragon had no choice but to break his promise to the villagers and interrupt his five-hundred-year-long slumber. He arose one night, too weak to fly, and walked back to his old cave on Eagle Mountain. His body was hurting and his heart was sad. He needed some time alone to nurse himself back to health.

但随着时间流逝，它逐渐失去龙的模样，越来越像一座普通的老石桥。于是桃花村的后辈子孙们，开始怀疑龙桥故事的真实性，认为那只是一则神话。甚至后来，完全忘记了整个故事的来龙去脉。最后，连一年一度的庆祝日也不再举行了。就这样几十年下来，龙桥开始被河泥和灰尘层层覆盖，直到后来再也无法令人想像到，它其实是一只真的龙。

这只沉睡了三百年的巨龙，终于在灼痛和骚痒中醒来。在缺乏村民的照顾下，它生病了。它发现桃花村的村民不但不再崇拜它，甚至把龙桥的存在当做理所当然。这一切使它别无选择，只能打破对他们的承诺，提早终止原本预计的五百年沉睡。它那天晚上醒来，身体虚弱得无法飞行，只能带着痛楚的身体和伤透了的心，勉强走回它原来的老洞，它需要一段时间来独自疗伤。

After listening to the dragon's sad tale, Master Chen took his leave and returned to the village. There he told the people the amazing story of the missing bridge and the plight of the unhappy dragon. The villagers all decided something must be done. So Old Lee came up with a plan.

The next day a group of villagers climbed up the mountain to the dragon's cave. There they bowed down before the mighty beast and begged his forgiveness. Then they set about giving him a good cleaning. After he was all bright and shiny again, the village doctor applied herbal medicines to treat his wounds. The dragon was very pleased by all the attention, and he began to look a little happier.

听完这巨龙悲伤的故事，陈师傅赶紧回到村子，告诉村民们山上有只受伤的龙，并说出有关这只龙与龙桥的神奇故事。村民们决定他们必须弥补一切，于是李长老想到一个计划。

　　第二天，村民们一起爬到巨龙所在的山洞口。他们对巨龙深深地鞠躬，并请求它的原谅。然后他们开始为它做彻底的清洗，又请来村里的医师用草药为它治疗伤口。很高兴村民对它如此重视，巨龙终于稍稍快乐了起来。

When the villagers finished, they again bowed before the great creature and begged him to return to the river. But he told them, sadly, that he could not. You see, once a dragon awakens from his hibernation, he cannot return to sleep again for another thousand years. However, the dragon was so touched by their show of kindness and remorse that he decided then and there to help them to build a new bridge. And so he did.

当他们完成之后，村民们再度向巨龍深深一鞠躬，并请求它再回去当龙桥，但是它哀伤地告诉他们，它已无能为力了，因为一只龙的沉睡一旦被打断，就无法再继续。但有感于村民的悔意和善待，巨龙决定帮他们建造一座新的桥，而且它真的做到了。

With the dragon's help, the villagers finished their new stone bridge just in time for the harvest season. Thus the farmers were able to take their peaches and almonds safely across the river to the market.

在巨龙的协助下，新的龙桥及时在中秋丰收前完成了。如此一来，农民们就可以准时带着他们的桃子和杏仁，安全地越过宝河，将农获运送到邻村的市集去。

Until this very day, the "new" Dragon Bridge still arches gracefully over the Po River at Peach Blossom Village in the shadow of Eagle Mountain. And each spring the villagers hold a festival to clean and polish their beautiful stone bridge, and they listen to the elders retell a strange tale about how it came to be built by a real dragon. As for the dragon, some say he returned to live among his own kind. But the village folk believe he still watches over them. And on the evening of the Dragon Festival, if you look very carefully, they say you can see him dancing on the western horizon, as the sun sets like an orange ball in a sea of clouds.

直到今天，新的龙桥仍旧优雅地横拱在大鹰山下，桃花村的宝河上。村民们把龙桥日订在每年的春天，在这一天，他们会为这座美丽的石桥清洗和抛光。然后，村子的长老们会为村民和孩子们，再细述一次龙桥的故事，并说明它为何是一座龙盖的桥。至于那只巨龙，有些人说它早已回去和它的龙族同住。 但也有人相信，它其实还在附近守护着桃花村的村民 。因为每年在龙桥日这一天 ，只要你多用点心，一定可以在火红的夕阳中，看到它就舞动在天边的彩霞里。

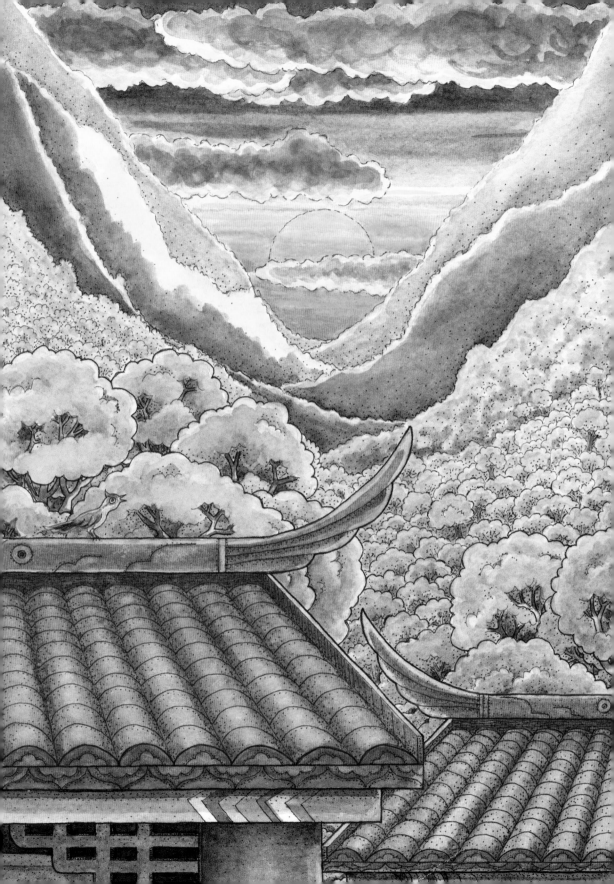

The End

About the Author

PHOTO BY KENT HOWARD

Ann Howard was born in a small town in "Butterfly Valley," deep in the mountains of Taiwan. She spent her childhood wandering the hillsides, chasing butterflies and dragonflies and sketching everything she saw. Howard has been a professional artist most of her adult life, painting surreal oils and watercolor illustrations. The Peach Blossom Village stories are a patchwork of her childhood memories interwoven with the landscape of her Northern California home. This is her first work of fiction. Find her online at www.annhowardstudio.com.